A Gift For:
[handwritten signature]
From:
[handwritten signature]

Editorial Director: Carrie Bolin
Editor: Kim Schworm Acosta
Art Director: Jan Mastin
Designer: Mary Eakin
Illustrator: Terry Runyan
Production Designer: Dan Horton
Writer: Diana Manning
Contributing Writers: Ellen Brenneman,
Bill Gray, and Molly Wigand

ISBN: 978-1-59530-836-8
BOK2184

Made in China
FEB16

Because you're my friend,
I have a whole heart full of wishes
just waiting to be wished for you.

Wow! Where do we start?

Let's start at the beginning.

Clear your thoughts of **have-to's**.
You deserve way more **want-to's**.

We've talked about the things
          that tend to worry us . . .

and friends don't let friends

stay stressed out.

You can count on me for that.

I wish you the freedom to
        think about what really makes you happy . . .

and then the freedom to do it!

Open road, top down, cool sunglasses,

and a **song from high school**
turned up loud.

A warm sun,
   a cool drink,
   a juicy read . . .

and a leisurely afternoon to enjoy them all.

May the **sweet taste of life**
linger on your tongue . . .

as well as the sweet taste of chocolate.

Expensive, imported chocolate.

Cavort a little.

The world needs more cavorting.

A little more

lightheartedness, too.

And how about some time . . .

the kind of carefree time
your **imagination** needs to really soar . . .

the kind your heart needs to create new dreams.

Find that quiet spot
to call your own,

and let the clouds
and the trees
and **the fresh air**
work their magic on you.

Reconnect with the kind of things

you used to love as a kid,

the kind of **pure joy**
you had when you were five
and swinging higher
than you ever had before.

Hope you'll feel inspired to try new things . . .

to reach for more.
    Because you inspire ME, you know.

I wish you
the chance

to **surprise** yourself . . .

to break out of your comfort zone (just a little)

and do something you once thought was so "not you."

I wish you the sense of accomplishment

that comes from walking a steep, winding trail . . .

braving the unknown . . .

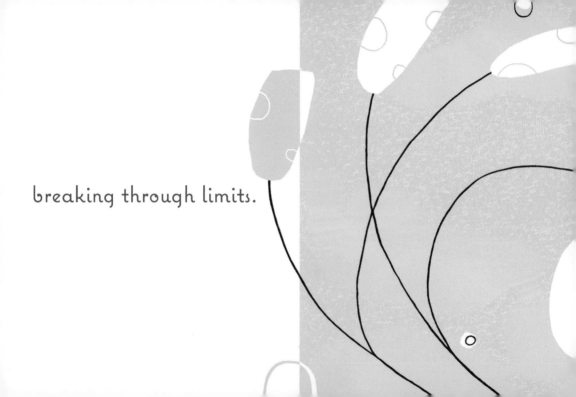

breaking through limits.

I wish you a moment of pure illumination

when something puzzling

finally makes perfect, beautiful sense.

Here's to all kinds
of **everyday goodness,** as well:

an awesome, flattering combo in your closet
that you never saw before,

a toothless grin from a baby,

a **punch line** delivered just right.

By all means, I hope every day

holds some words of appreciation

and that you hear them

loud and clear and boisterously

from every little corner of your world.

May **it** come . . .

the letter, the text, the voice
that says what you've been

longing to hear . . .

or the unexpected one

that says something **even better.**

You deserve to hear **good things,** after all.

Put the modesty on hold
         just long enough to see yourself
                  as others see you.

Take a moment to remember

that you are often the highlight of someone's day

and the answer to someone's prayer.

So for all you are to others,

may the world always be kind to you . . .

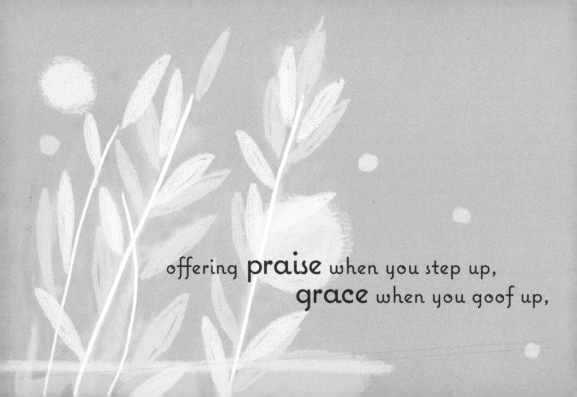

offering **praise** when you step up,
grace when you goof up,

and **love** . . . just because you're you.

And may you know

that even if **all these wishes** come true,

my heart still has **more for you.**

I'll always be hoping
        for life's best things for you . . .

my wonderful, warmhearted friend!

If you have enjoyed this book
or it has touched your life in some way,
we would love to hear from you.

Please send your comments to:
Hallmark Book Feedback
P.O. Box 419034
Mail Drop 100
Kansas City, MO 64141

Or e-mail us at:
booknotes@hallmark.com